STAR WARS®

THE CLONE WARS™

SLAVES OF THE REPUBLIC
VOLUME FOUR

"AUCTION OF A MILLION SOULS"

SCRIPT
HENRY GILROY

PENCILS
SCOTT HEPBURN

INKS
DAN PARSONS

COLORS
MICHAEL E. WIGGAM

LETTERING
MICHAEL HEISLER

COVER ART
SCOTT HEPBURN AND RONDA PATTISON

Anakin, Obi-Wan, Ahsoka, and Rex have infiltrated the homeworld of the Zygerrians, the most vicious slavers in the galaxy. Desperate to locate the vanished population of Togruta colonists, the Jedi masquerade as slavers to attend an epic slave auction, where they believe the missing people will be sold into bondage.

Anakin wins the favor of the Zygerrian Queen by giving her his "slave," Ahsoka—who is posing as a kidnapped princess. Attracted to the roguishly disguised Jedi, the Queen grants him a place at her side for the auction.

Meanwhile, Obi-Wan is captured trying to rescue the leader of the missing Togruta from the palace dungeon, throwing the Jedi's plans into disarray . . .

DARK HORSE COMICS

Spotlight

VISIT US AT
www.abdopublishing.com

Reinforced library bound edition published in 2010 by Spotlight, a division of the ABDO Group, 8000 West 78th Street, Edina, Minnesota 55439. Spotlight produces high-quality reinforced library bound editions for schools and libraries. Published by agreement with Dark Horse Comics, Inc., and Lucasfilm Ltd.

Printed in the United States of America, Melrose Park, Illinois.
092009
012010

 PRINTED ON RECYCLED PAPER

Library of Congress Cataloging-in-Publication Data

Gilroy, Henry.
  Slaves of the republic / script by Henry Gilroy ; pencils by Scott Hepburn ; inks by Dan Parsons ; colors by Michael E. Wiggam ; lettering by Michael Heisler.
-- Reinforced library bound ed.
     v. cm. -- (Star wars: the clone wars)
  "Dark Horse Comics."
  Contents: v. 1. The mystery of Kiros -- v. 2. Slave traders of Zygerria -- v. 3. The depths of Zygerria -- v. 4. Auction of a million souls -- v. 5. A slave now, a slave forever -- v. 6. Escape from kadavo.
  ISBN 978-1-59961-710-7 (v. 1) -- ISBN 978-1-59961-711-4 (v. 2) -- ISBN 978-1-59961-712-1 (v. 3) -- ISBN 978-1-59961-713-8 (v. 4) -- ISBN 978-1-59961-714-5 (v. 5) -- ISBN 978-1-59961-715-2 (v. 6)
  1. Graphic novels. [1. Graphic novels.] I. Hepburn, Scott. II. Star Wars, the clone wars (Television program) III. Title.
  PZ7.7.G55Sl 2010
  [Fic]--dc22
                              2009030553

All Spotlight books have reinforced library bindings and are manufactured in the United States of America.

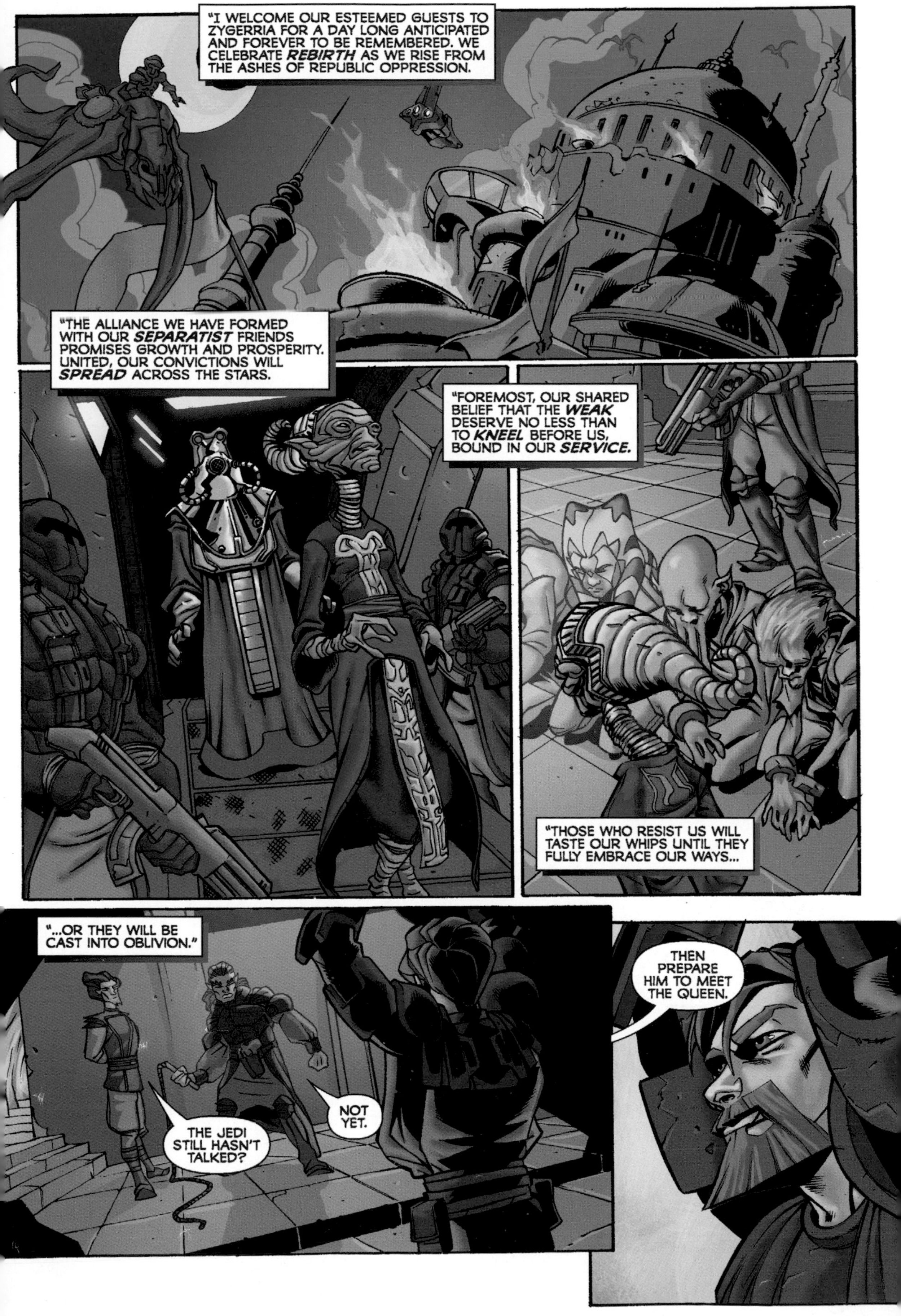
"I WELCOME OUR ESTEEMED GUESTS TO ZYGERRIA FOR A DAY LONG ANTICIPATED AND FOREVER TO BE REMEMBERED. WE CELEBRATE REBIRTH AS WE RISE FROM THE ASHES OF REPUBLIC OPPRESSION.
"THE ALLIANCE WE HAVE FORMED WITH OUR SEPARATIST FRIENDS PROMISES GROWTH AND PROSPERITY. UNITED, OUR CONVICTIONS WILL SPREAD ACROSS THE STARS.
"FOREMOST, OUR SHARED BELIEF THAT THE WEAK DESERVE NO LESS THAN TO KNEEL BEFORE US, BOUND IN OUR SERVICE.
"THOSE WHO RESIST US WILL TASTE OUR WHIPS UNTIL THEY FULLY EMBRACE OUR WAYS...
"...OR THEY WILL BE CAST INTO OBLIVION."
THE JEDI STILL HASN'T TALKED?
NOT YET.
THEN PREPARE HIM TO MEET THE QUEEN.

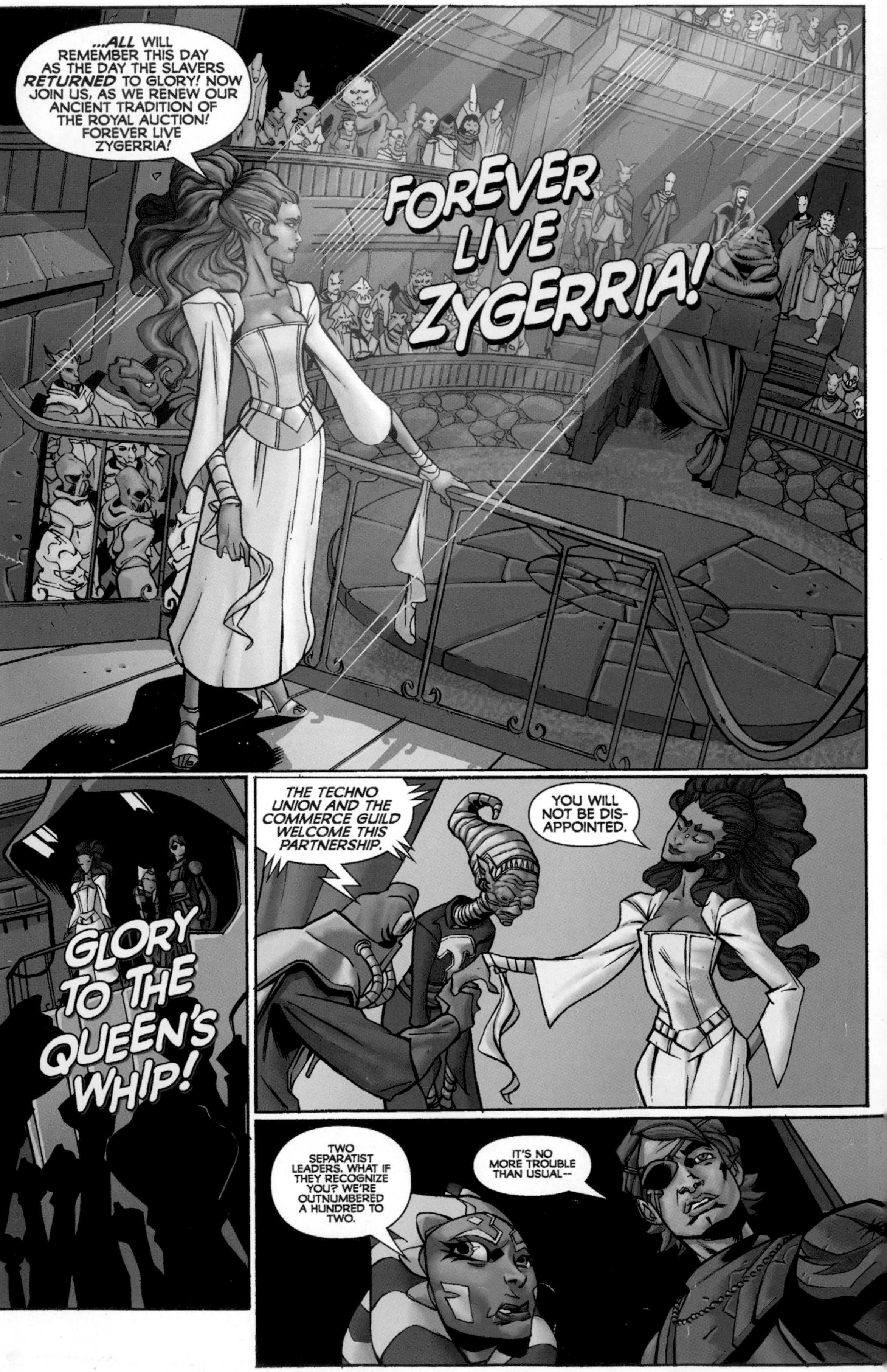
...ALL WILL REMEMBER THIS DAY AS THE DAY THE SLAVERS RETURNED TO GLORY! NOW JOIN US, AS WE RENEW OUR ANCIENT TRADITION OF THE ROYAL AUCTION! FOREVER LIVE ZYGERRIA!
FOREVER LIVE ZYGERRIA!
GLORY TO THE QUEEN'S WHIP!
THE TECHNO UNION AND THE COMMERCE GUILD WELCOME THIS PARTNERSHIP.
YOU WILL NOT BE DIS-APPOINTED.
TWO SEPARATIST LEADERS. WHAT IF THEY RECOGNIZE YOU? WE'RE OUTNUMBERED A HUNDRED TO TWO.
IT'S NO MORE TROUBLE THAN USUAL--

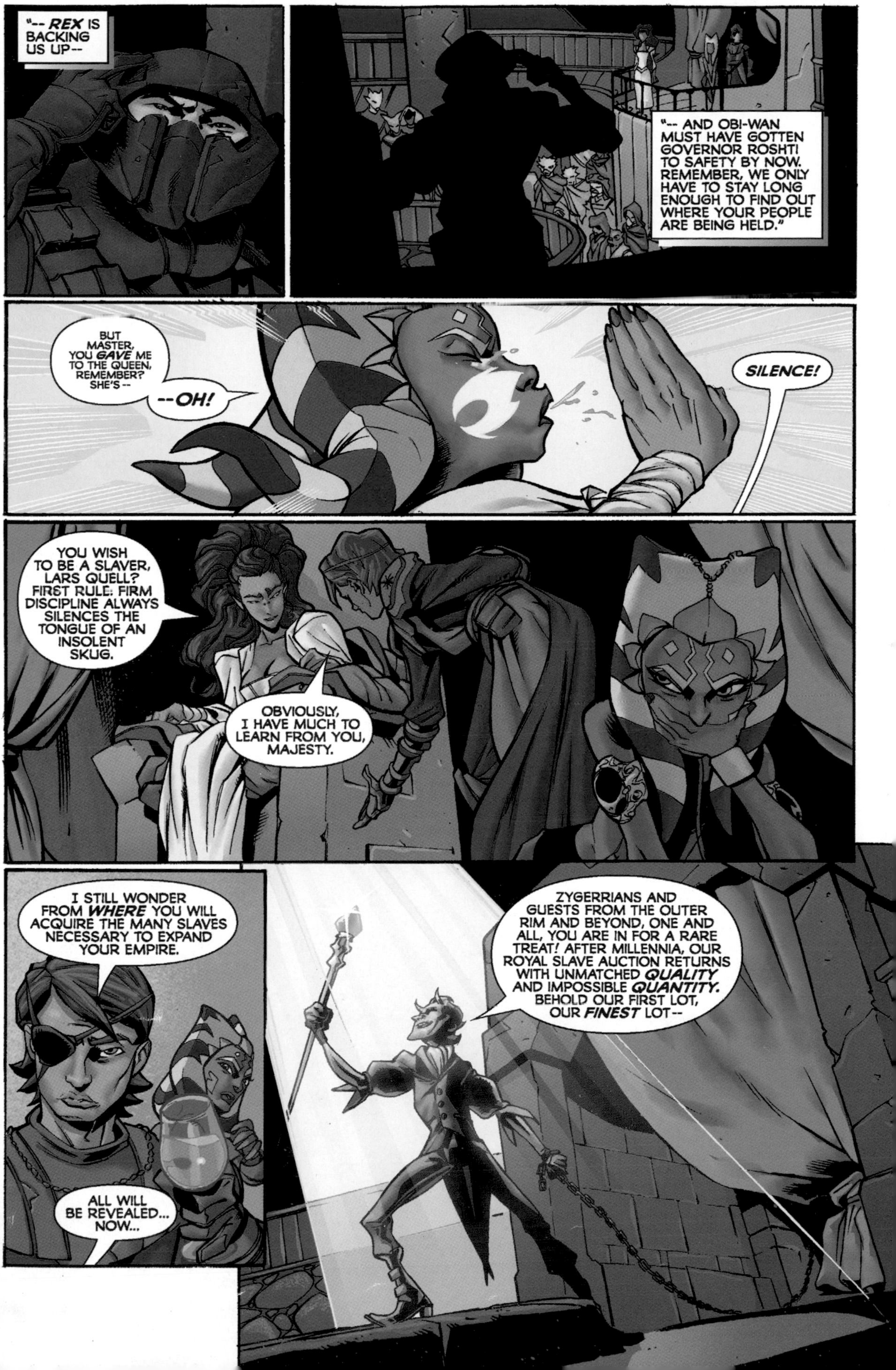
"-- REX IS BACKING US UP--
"-- AND OBI-WAN MUST HAVE GOTTEN GOVERNOR ROSHTI TO SAFETY BY NOW. REMEMBER, WE ONLY HAVE TO STAY LONG ENOUGH TO FIND OUT WHERE YOUR PEOPLE ARE BEING HELD."
BUT MASTER, YOU GAVE ME TO THE QUEEN, REMEMBER? SHE'S --
--OH!
SILENCE!
YOU WISH TO BE A SLAVER, LARS QUELL? FIRST RULE: FIRM DISCIPLINE ALWAYS SILENCES THE TONGUE OF AN INSOLENT SKUG.
OBVIOUSLY, I HAVE MUCH TO LEARN FROM YOU, MAJESTY.
I STILL WONDER FROM WHERE YOU WILL ACQUIRE THE MANY SLAVES NECESSARY TO EXPAND YOUR EMPIRE.
ALL WILL BE REVEALED... NOW...
ZYGERRIANS AND GUESTS FROM THE OUTER RIM AND BEYOND, ONE AND ALL, YOU ARE IN FOR A RARE TREAT! AFTER MILLENNIA, OUR ROYAL SLAVE AUCTION RETURNS WITH UNMATCHED QUALITY AND IMPOSSIBLE QUANTITY. BEHOLD OUR FIRST LOT, OUR FINEST LOT--

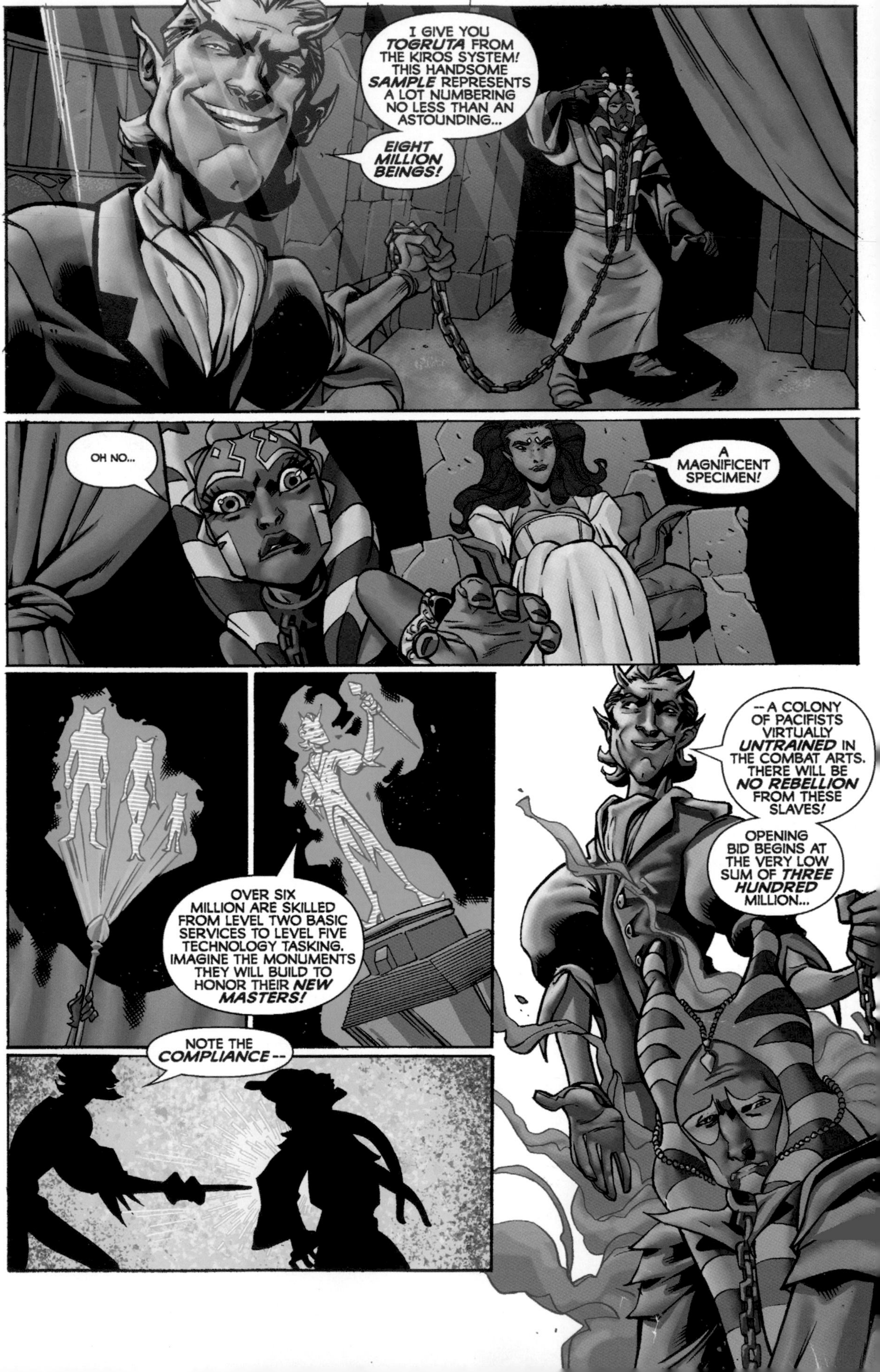
I GIVE YOU *TOGRUTA* FROM THE KIROS SYSTEM! THIS HANDSOME *SAMPLE* REPRESENTS A LOT NUMBERING NO LESS THAN AN ASTOUNDING...
EIGHT MILLION BEINGS!
OH NO...
A MAGNIFICENT SPECIMEN!
OVER SIX MILLION ARE SKILLED FROM LEVEL TWO BASIC SERVICES TO LEVEL FIVE TECHNOLOGY TASKING. IMAGINE THE MONUMENTS THEY WILL BUILD TO HONOR THEIR *NEW MASTERS!*
NOTE THE *COMPLIANCE* --
-- A COLONY OF PACIFISTS VIRTUALLY *UNTRAINED* IN THE COMBAT ARTS. THERE WILL BE *NO REBELLION* FROM THESE SLAVES!
OPENING BID BEGINS AT THE VERY LOW SUM OF *THREE HUNDRED* MILLION...

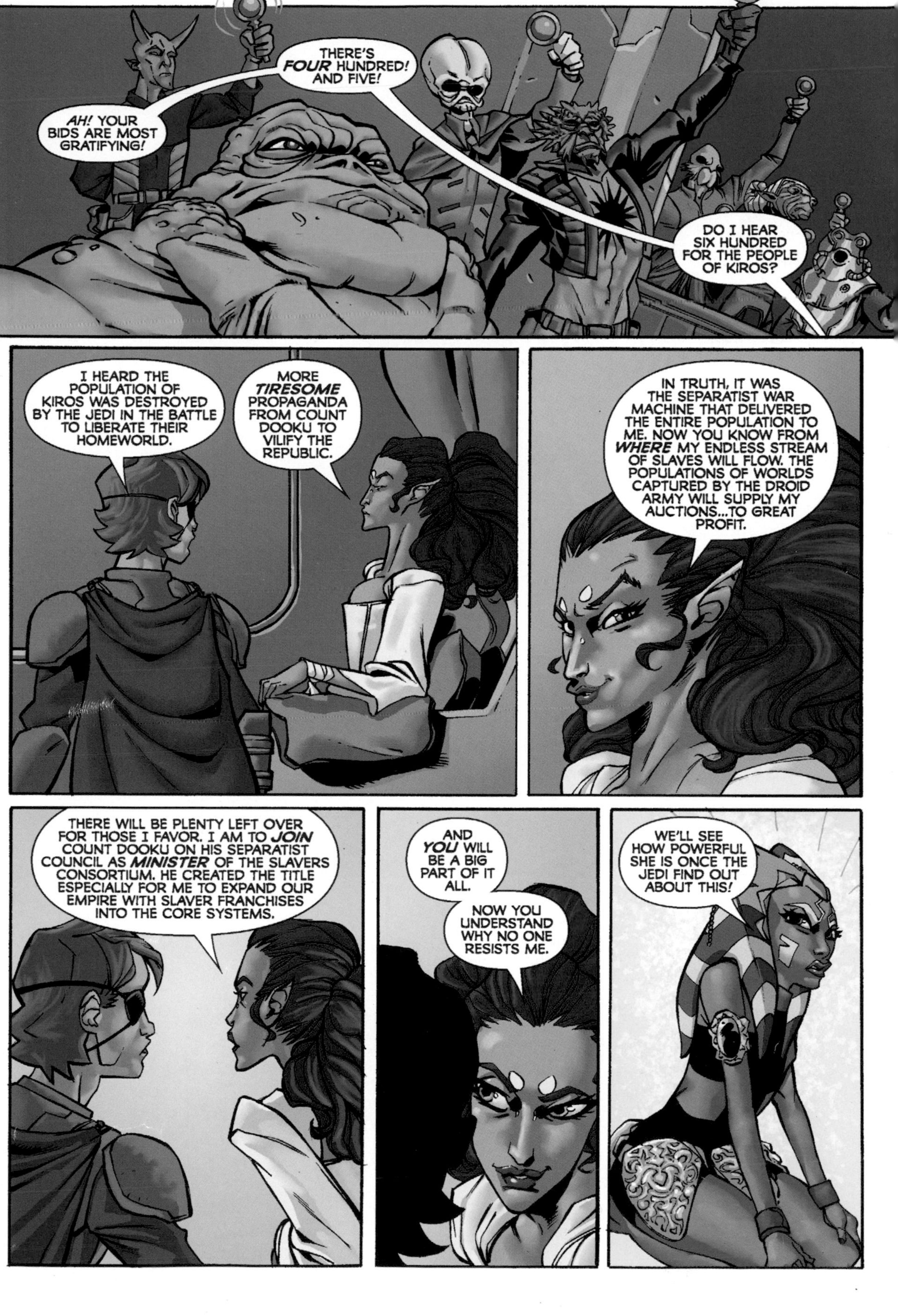
AH! YOUR BIDS ARE MOST GRATIFYING!
THERE'S FOUR HUNDRED! AND FIVE!
DO I HEAR SIX HUNDRED FOR THE PEOPLE OF KIROS?
I HEARD THE POPULATION OF KIROS WAS DESTROYED BY THE JEDI IN THE BATTLE TO LIBERATE THEIR HOMEWORLD.
MORE TIRESOME PROPAGANDA FROM COUNT DOOKU TO VILIFY THE REPUBLIC.
IN TRUTH, IT WAS THE SEPARATIST WAR MACHINE THAT DELIVERED THE ENTIRE POPULATION TO ME. NOW YOU KNOW FROM WHERE MY ENDLESS STREAM OF SLAVES WILL FLOW. THE POPULATIONS OF WORLDS CAPTURED BY THE DROID ARMY WILL SUPPLY MY AUCTIONS...TO GREAT PROFIT.
THERE WILL BE PLENTY LEFT OVER FOR THOSE I FAVOR. I AM TO JOIN COUNT DOOKU ON HIS SEPARATIST COUNCIL AS MINISTER OF THE SLAVERS CONSORTIUM. HE CREATED THE TITLE ESPECIALLY FOR ME TO EXPAND OUR EMPIRE WITH SLAVER FRANCHISES INTO THE CORE SYSTEMS.
AND YOU WILL BE A BIG PART OF IT ALL.
NOW YOU UNDERSTAND WHY NO ONE RESISTS ME.
WE'LL SEE HOW POWERFUL SHE IS ONCE THE JEDI FIND OUT ABOUT THIS!

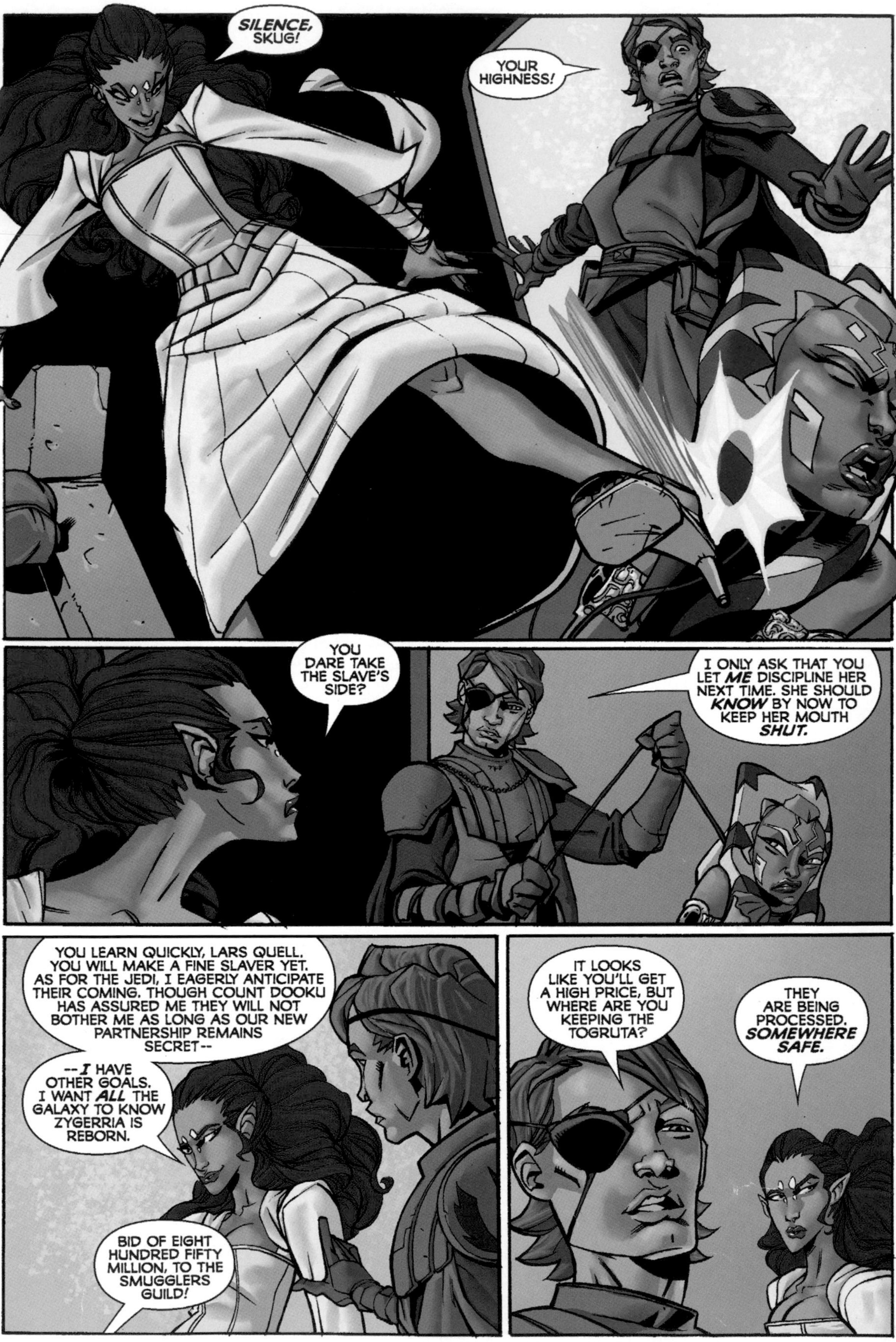
SILENCE, SKUG!
YOUR HIGHNESS!
YOU DARE TAKE THE SLAVE'S SIDE?
I ONLY ASK THAT YOU LET ME DISCIPLINE HER NEXT TIME. SHE SHOULD KNOW BY NOW TO KEEP HER MOUTH SHUT.
YOU LEARN QUICKLY, LARS QUELL. YOU WILL MAKE A FINE SLAVER YET. AS FOR THE JEDI, I EAGERLY ANTICIPATE THEIR COMING. THOUGH COUNT DOOKU HAS ASSURED ME THEY WILL NOT BOTHER ME AS LONG AS OUR NEW PARTNERSHIP REMAINS SECRET--
--I HAVE OTHER GOALS. I WANT ALL THE GALAXY TO KNOW ZYGERRIA IS REBORN.
BID OF EIGHT HUNDRED FIFTY MILLION, TO THE SMUGGLERS GUILD!
IT LOOKS LIKE YOU'LL GET A HIGH PRICE, BUT WHERE ARE YOU KEEPING THE TOGRUTA?
THEY ARE BEING PROCESSED. SOMEWHERE SAFE.

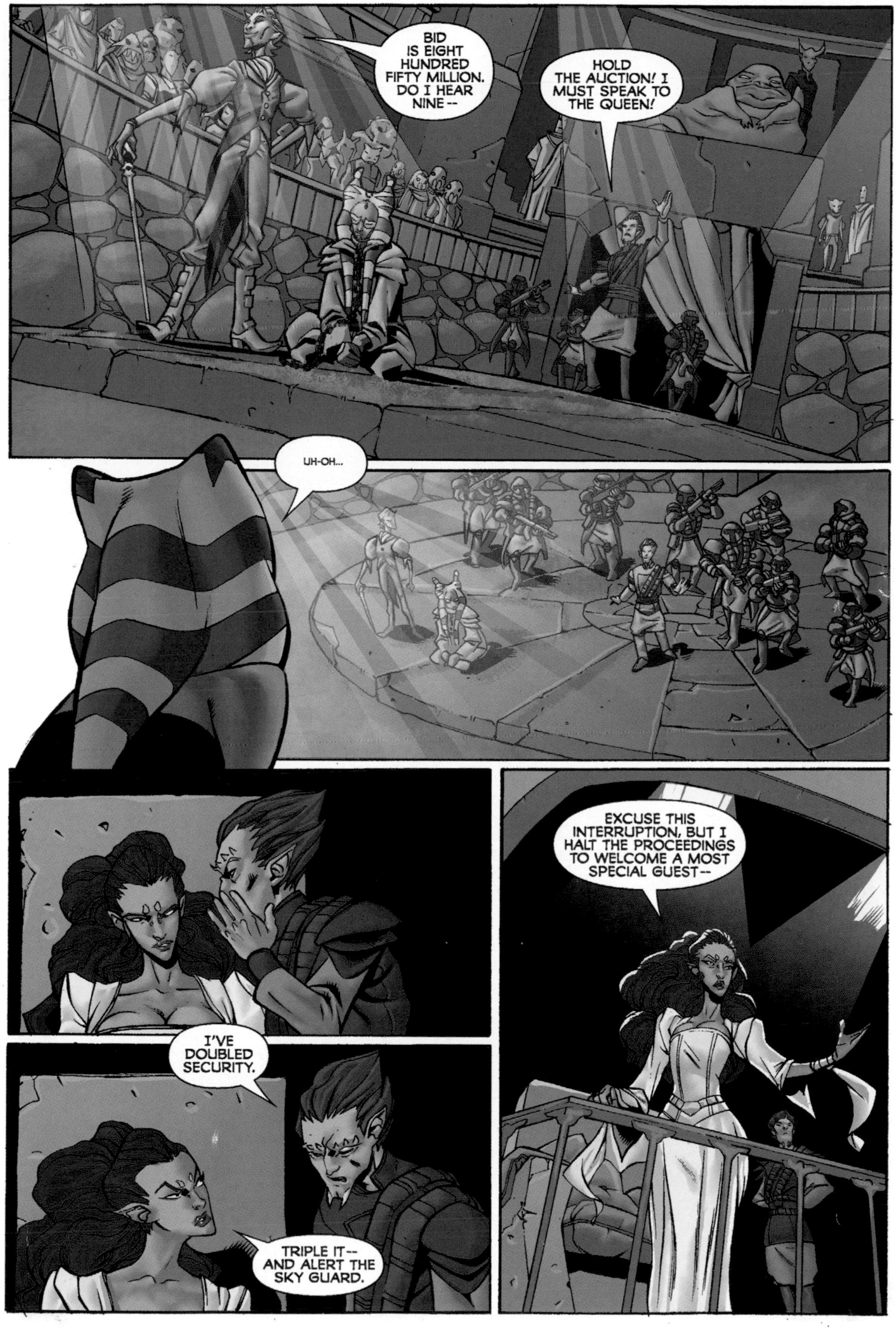
BID IS EIGHT HUNDRED FIFTY MILLION. DO I HEAR NINE--
HOLD THE AUCTION! I MUST SPEAK TO THE QUEEN!
UH-OH...
I'VE DOUBLED SECURITY.
TRIPLE IT-- AND ALERT THE SKY GUARD.
EXCUSE THIS INTERRUPTION, BUT I HALT THE PROCEEDINGS TO WELCOME A MOST SPECIAL GUEST--

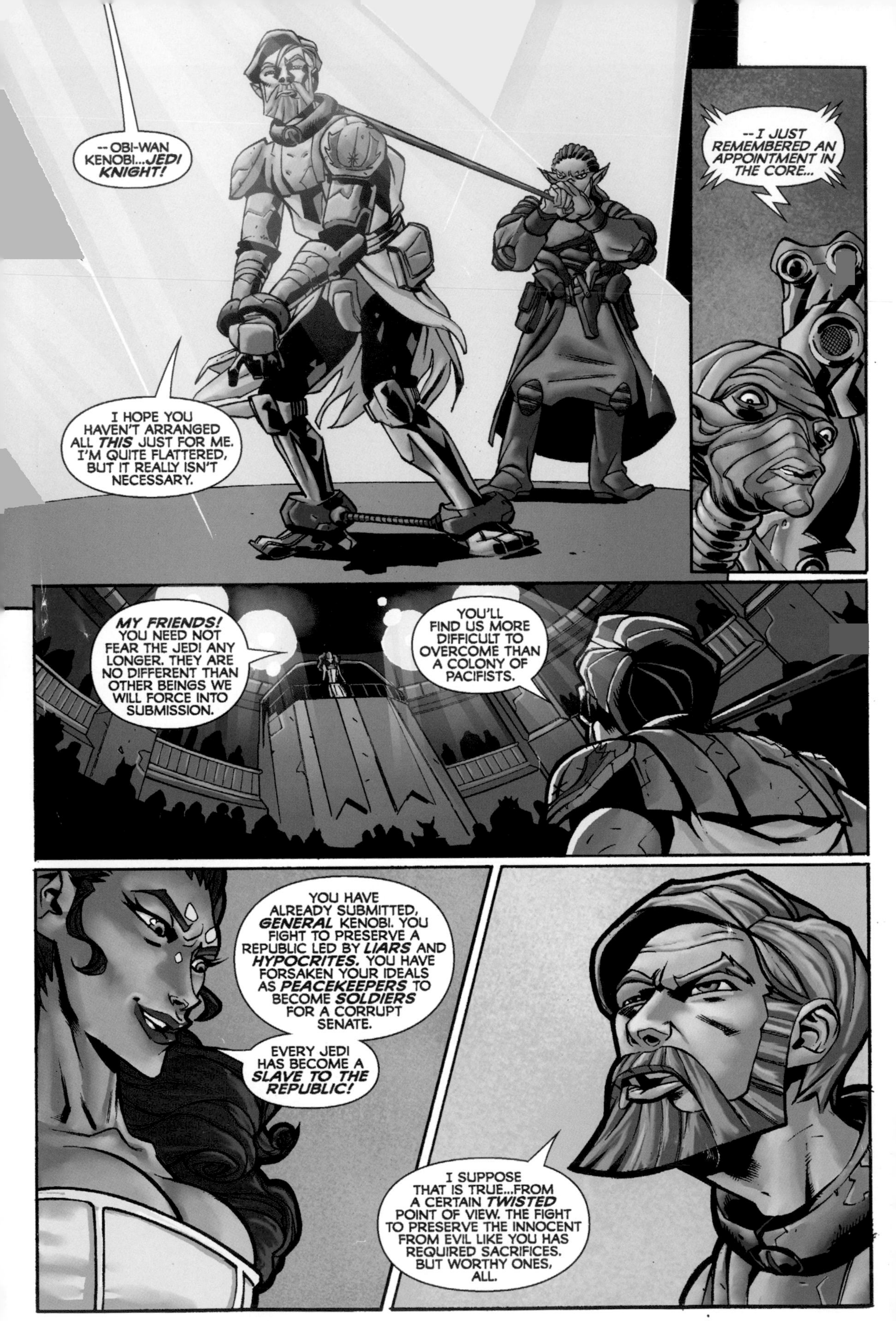
--OBI-WAN KENOBI...JEDI KNIGHT!
--I JUST REMEMBERED AN APPOINTMENT IN THE CORE...
I HOPE YOU HAVEN'T ARRANGED ALL THIS JUST FOR ME. I'M QUITE FLATTERED, BUT IT REALLY ISN'T NECESSARY.
MY FRIENDS! YOU NEED NOT FEAR THE JEDI ANY LONGER. THEY ARE NO DIFFERENT THAN OTHER BEINGS WE WILL FORCE INTO SUBMISSION.
YOU'LL FIND US MORE DIFFICULT TO OVERCOME THAN A COLONY OF PACIFISTS.
YOU HAVE ALREADY SUBMITTED, GENERAL KENOBI. YOU FIGHT TO PRESERVE A REPUBLIC LED BY LIARS AND HYPOCRITES. YOU HAVE FORSAKEN YOUR IDEALS AS PEACEKEEPERS TO BECOME SOLDIERS FOR A CORRUPT SENATE.
EVERY JEDI HAS BECOME A SLAVE TO THE REPUBLIC!
I SUPPOSE THAT IS TRUE...FROM A CERTAIN TWISTED POINT OF VIEW. THE FIGHT TO PRESERVE THE INNOCENT FROM EVIL LIKE YOU HAS REQUIRED SACRIFICES. BUT WORTHY ONES, ALL.

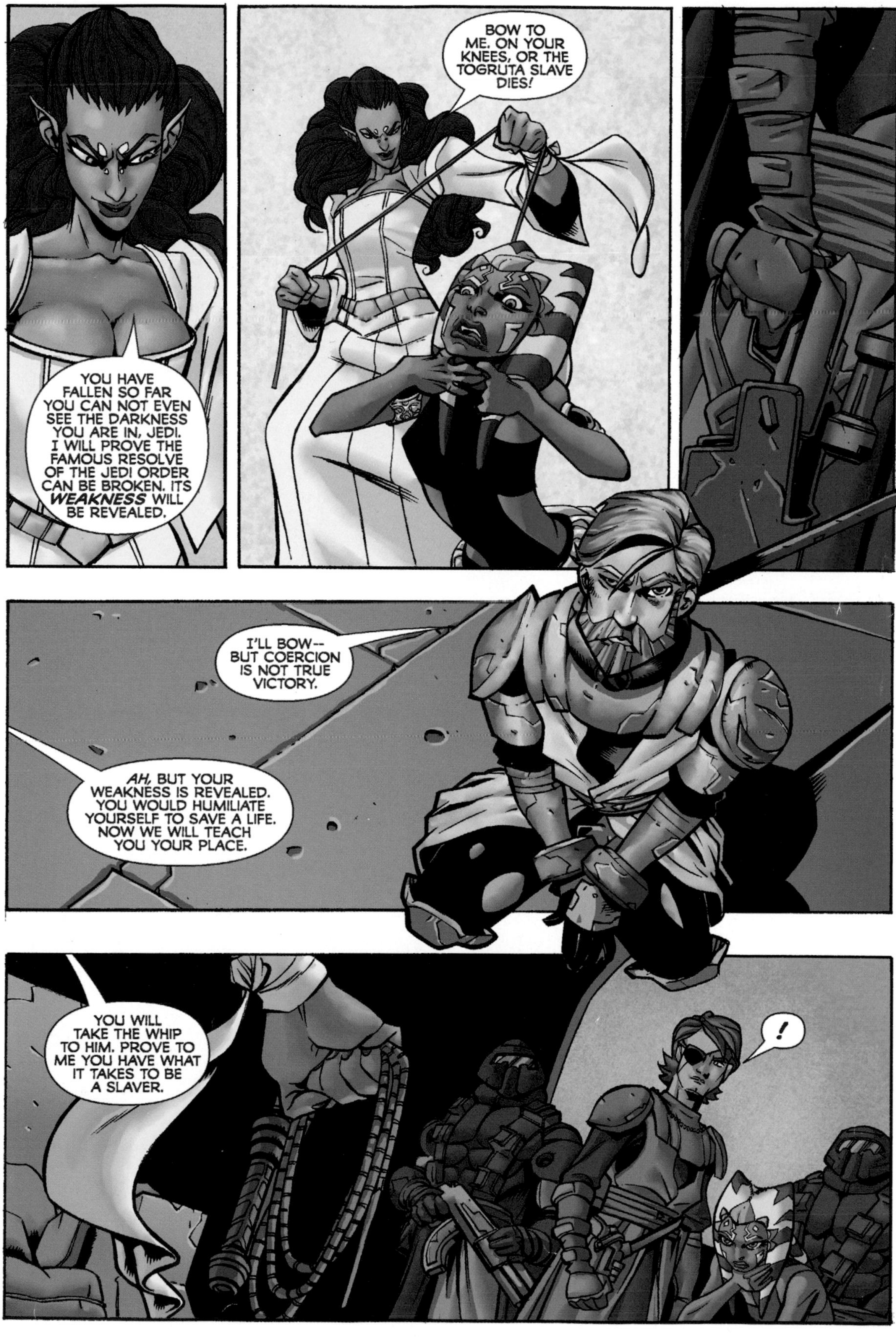
YOU HAVE FALLEN SO FAR YOU CAN NOT EVEN SEE THE DARKNESS YOU ARE IN, JEDI. I WILL PROVE THE FAMOUS RESOLVE OF THE JEDI ORDER CAN BE BROKEN. ITS *WEAKNESS* WILL BE REVEALED.
BOW TO ME. ON YOUR KNEES, OR THE TOGRUTA SLAVE DIES!
I'LL BOW-- BUT COERCION IS NOT TRUE VICTORY.
AH, BUT YOUR WEAKNESS IS REVEALED. YOU WOULD HUMILIATE YOURSELF TO SAVE A LIFE. NOW WE WILL TEACH YOU YOUR PLACE.
YOU WILL TAKE THE WHIP TO HIM. PROVE TO ME YOU HAVE WHAT IT TAKES TO BE A SLAVER.
!

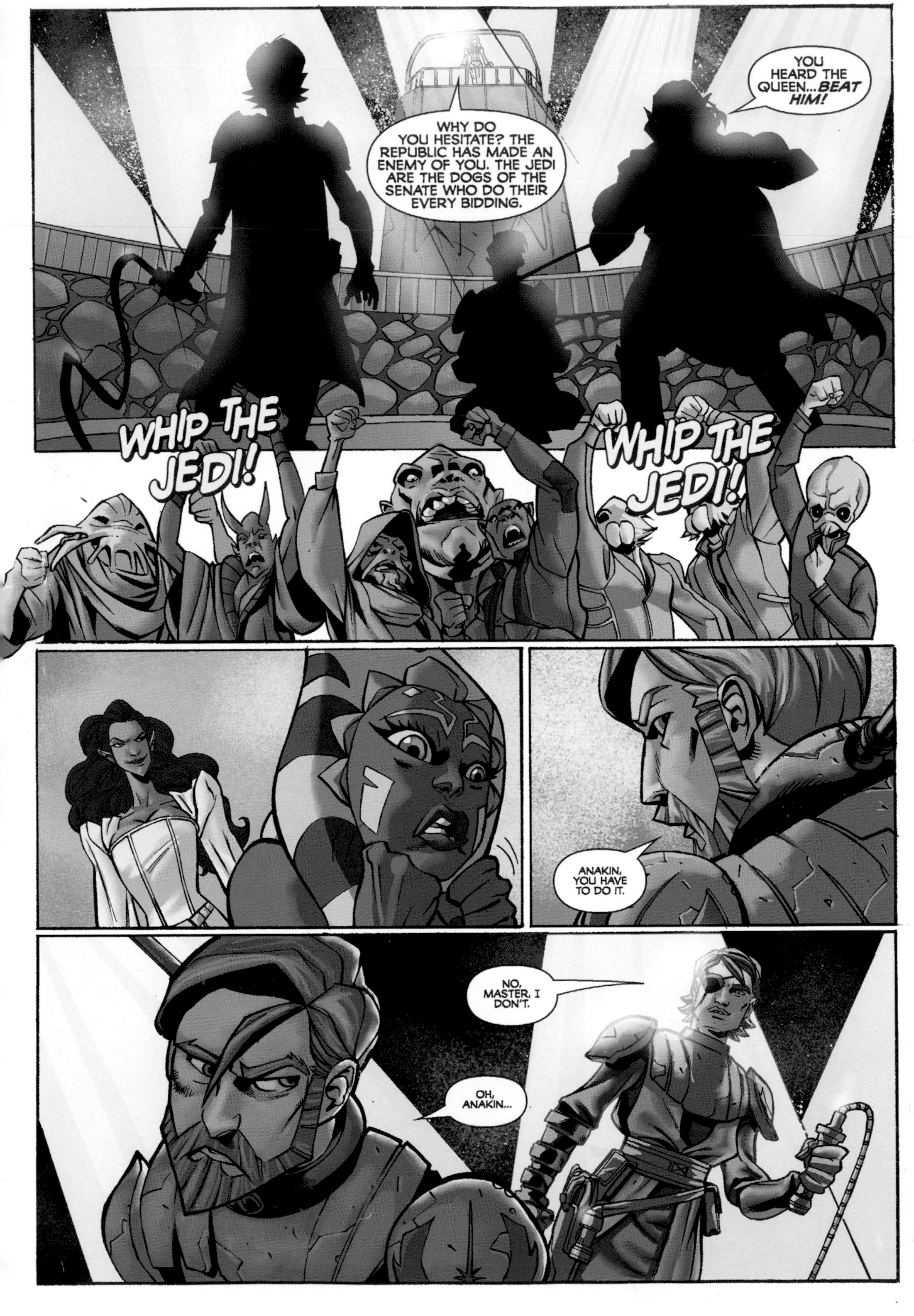
WHY DO YOU HESITATE? THE REPUBLIC HAS MADE AN ENEMY OF YOU. THE JEDI ARE THE DOGS OF THE SENATE WHO DO THEIR EVERY BIDDING.
YOU HEARD THE QUEEN...BEAT HIM!
WHIP THE JEDI!
WHIP THE JEDI!
ANAKIN, YOU HAVE TO DO IT.
NO, MASTER, I DON'T.
OH, ANAKIN...

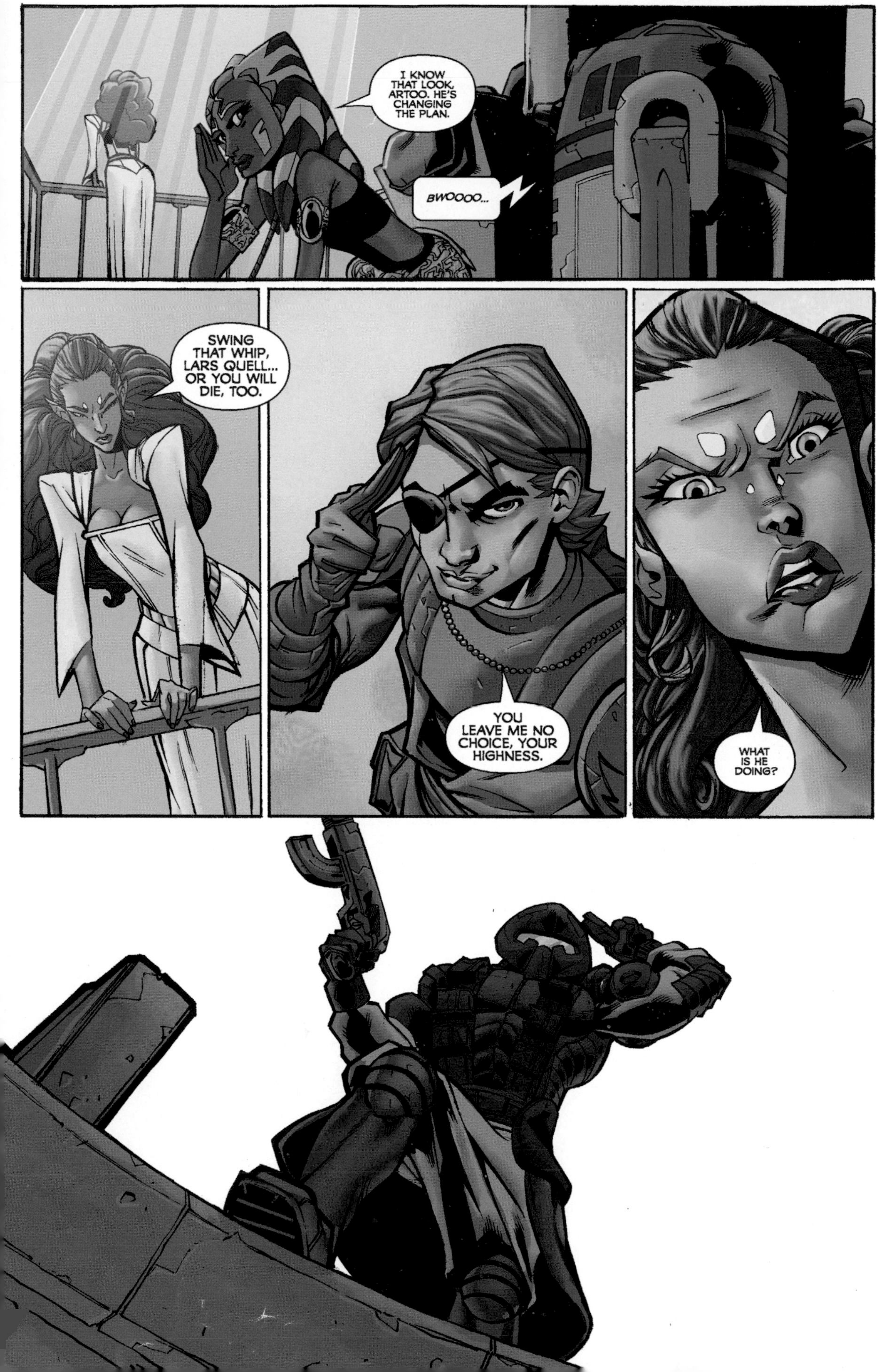
I KNOW THAT LOOK, ARTOO. HE'S CHANGING THE PLAN.
BWOOOO...
SWING THAT WHIP, LARS QUELL... OR YOU WILL DIE, TOO.
YOU LEAVE ME NO CHOICE, YOUR HIGHNESS.
WHAT IS HE DOING?

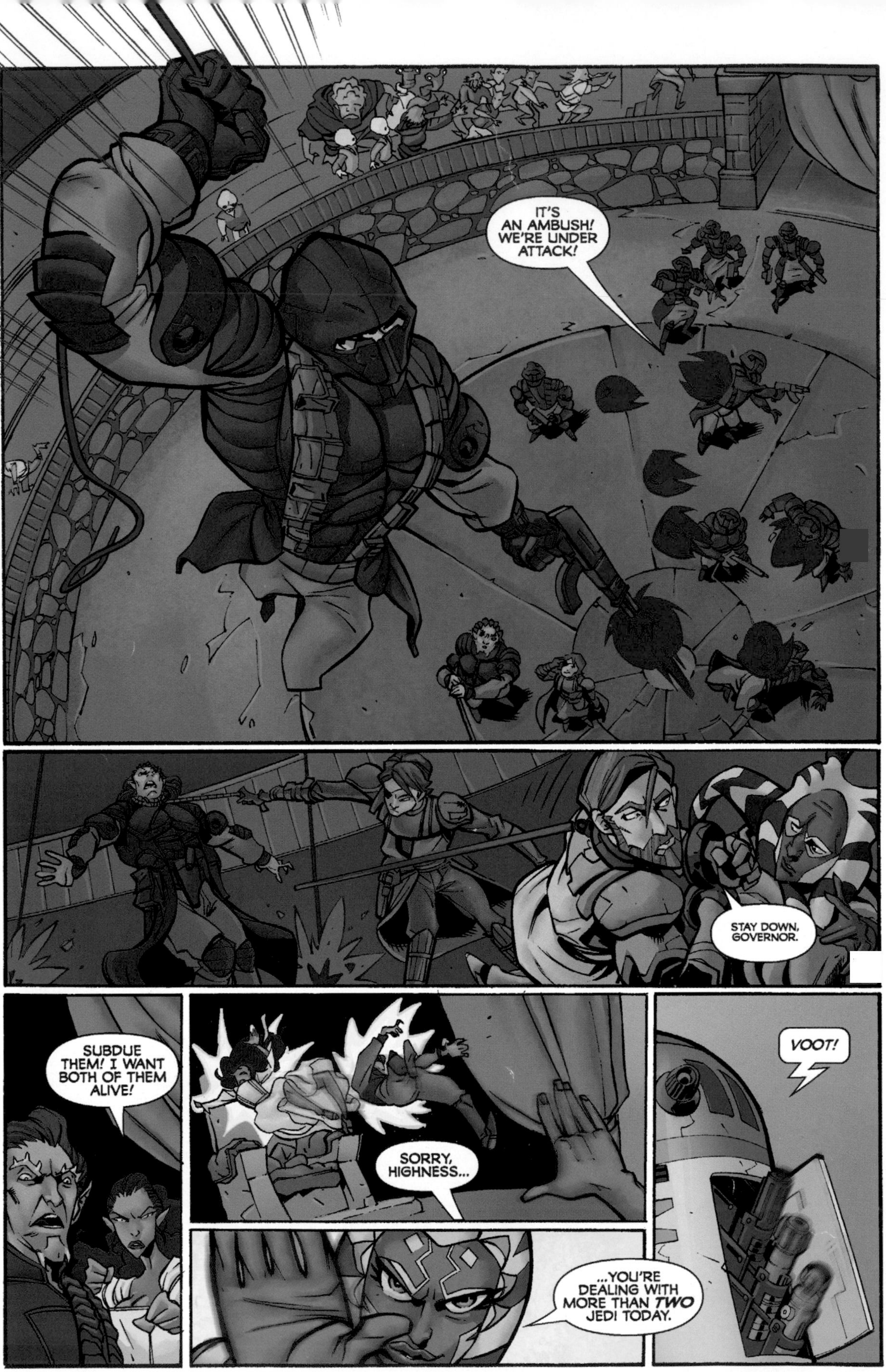
IT'S AN AMBUSH! WE'RE UNDER ATTACK!
STAY DOWN, GOVERNOR.
SUBDUE THEM! I WANT BOTH OF THEM ALIVE!
SORRY, HIGHNESS...
...YOU'RE DEALING WITH MORE THAN TWO JEDI TODAY.
VOOT!

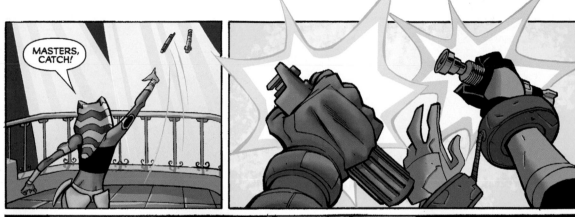

MASTERS, CATCH!

ANAKIN, WE HAVEN'T MUCH TIME!

I KNOW! LET'S GET THOSE CUFFS OFF OF YOU!

AHSOKA, TAKE THE QUEEN!

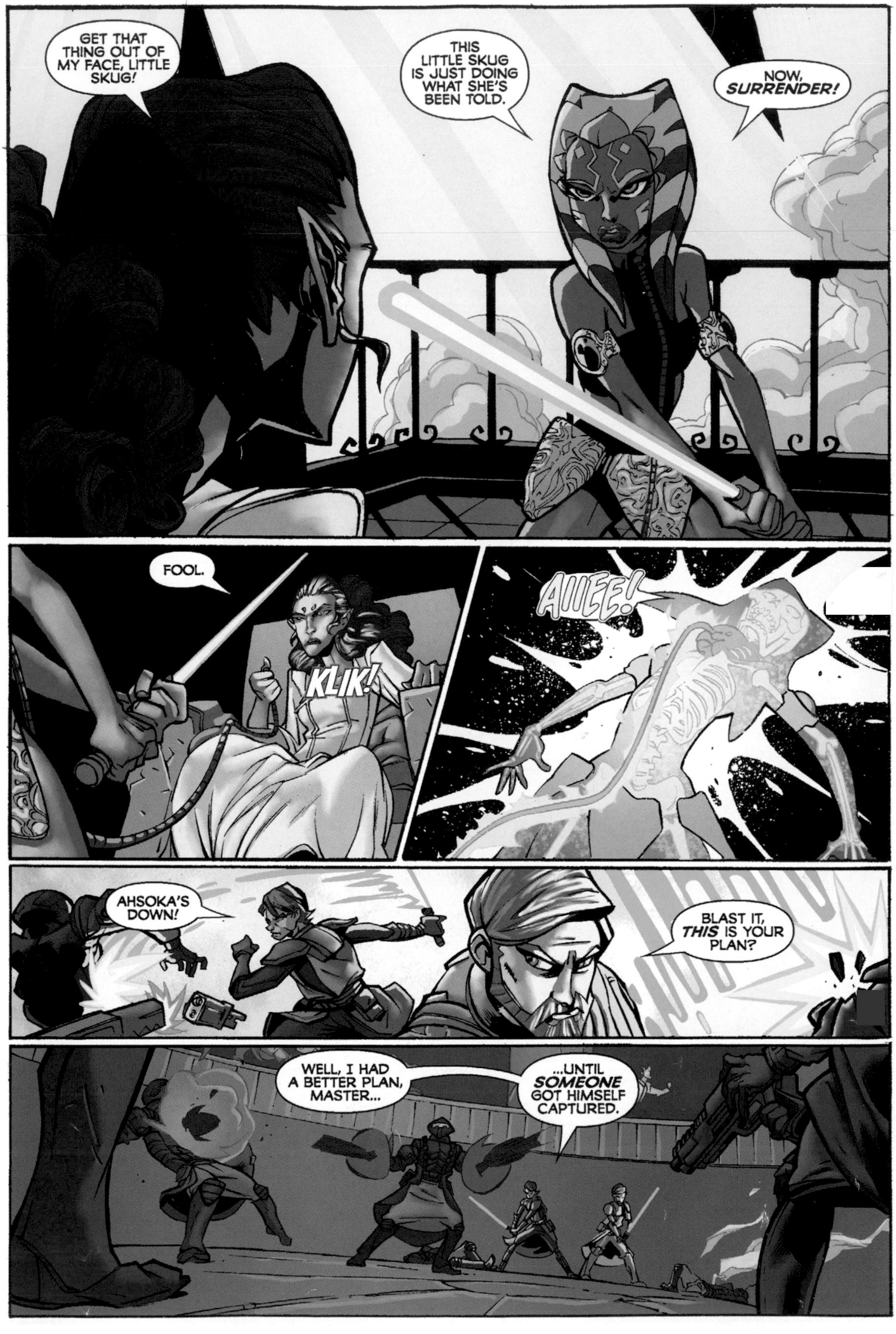
GET THAT THING OUT OF MY FACE, LITTLE SKUG!
THIS LITTLE SKUG IS JUST DOING WHAT SHE'S BEEN TOLD.
NOW, *SURRENDER!*
FOOL.
KLIK!
AIIEE!
AHSOKA'S DOWN!
BLAST IT, *THIS* IS YOUR PLAN?
WELL, I HAD A BETTER PLAN, MASTER...
...UNTIL *SOMEONE* GOT HIMSELF CAPTURED.

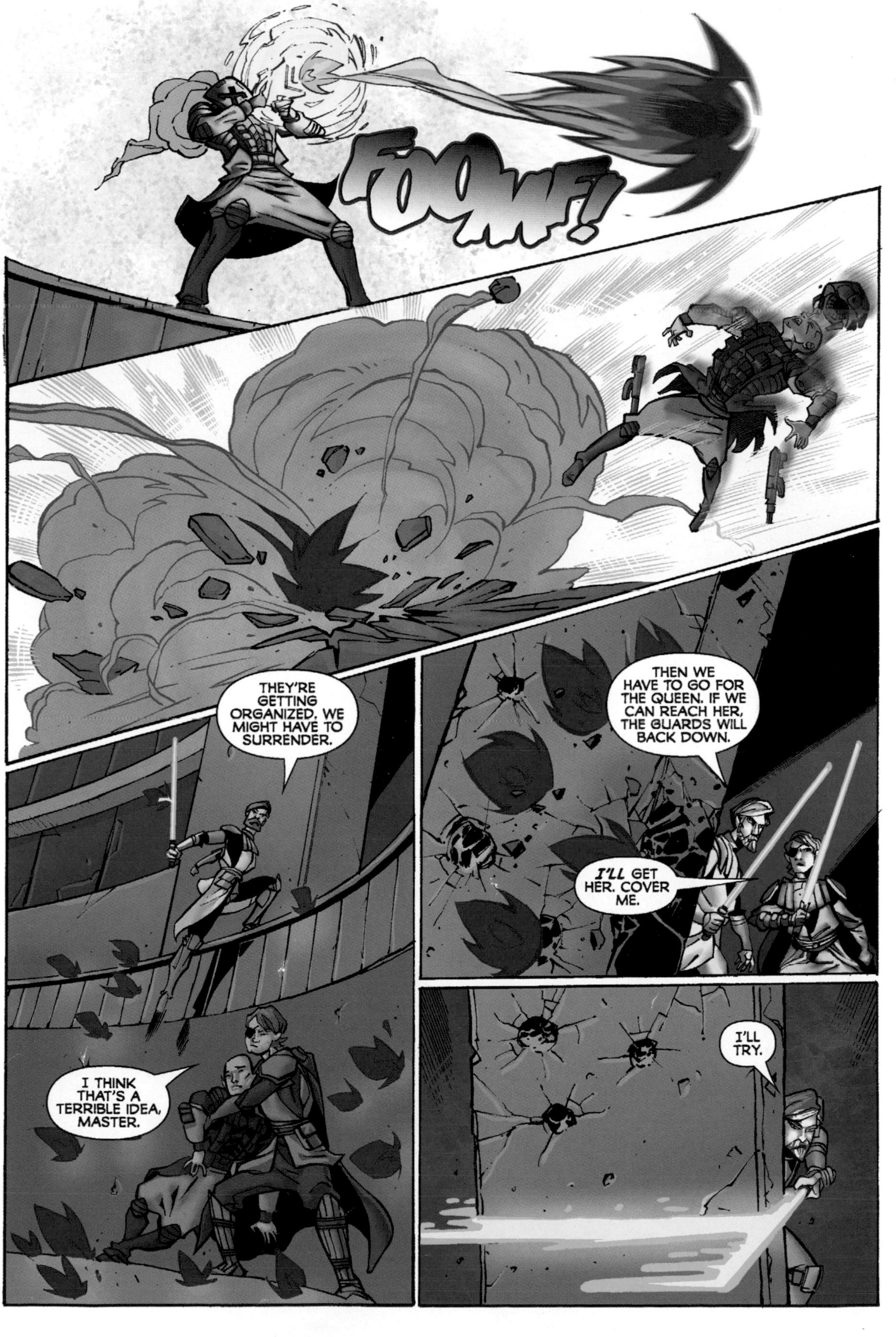
FOOMF!
THEY'RE GETTING ORGANIZED. WE MIGHT HAVE TO SURRENDER.
THEN WE HAVE TO GO FOR THE QUEEN. IF WE CAN REACH HER, THE GUARDS WILL BACK DOWN.
I'LL GET HER. COVER ME.
I THINK THAT'S A TERRIBLE IDEA, MASTER.
I'LL TRY.

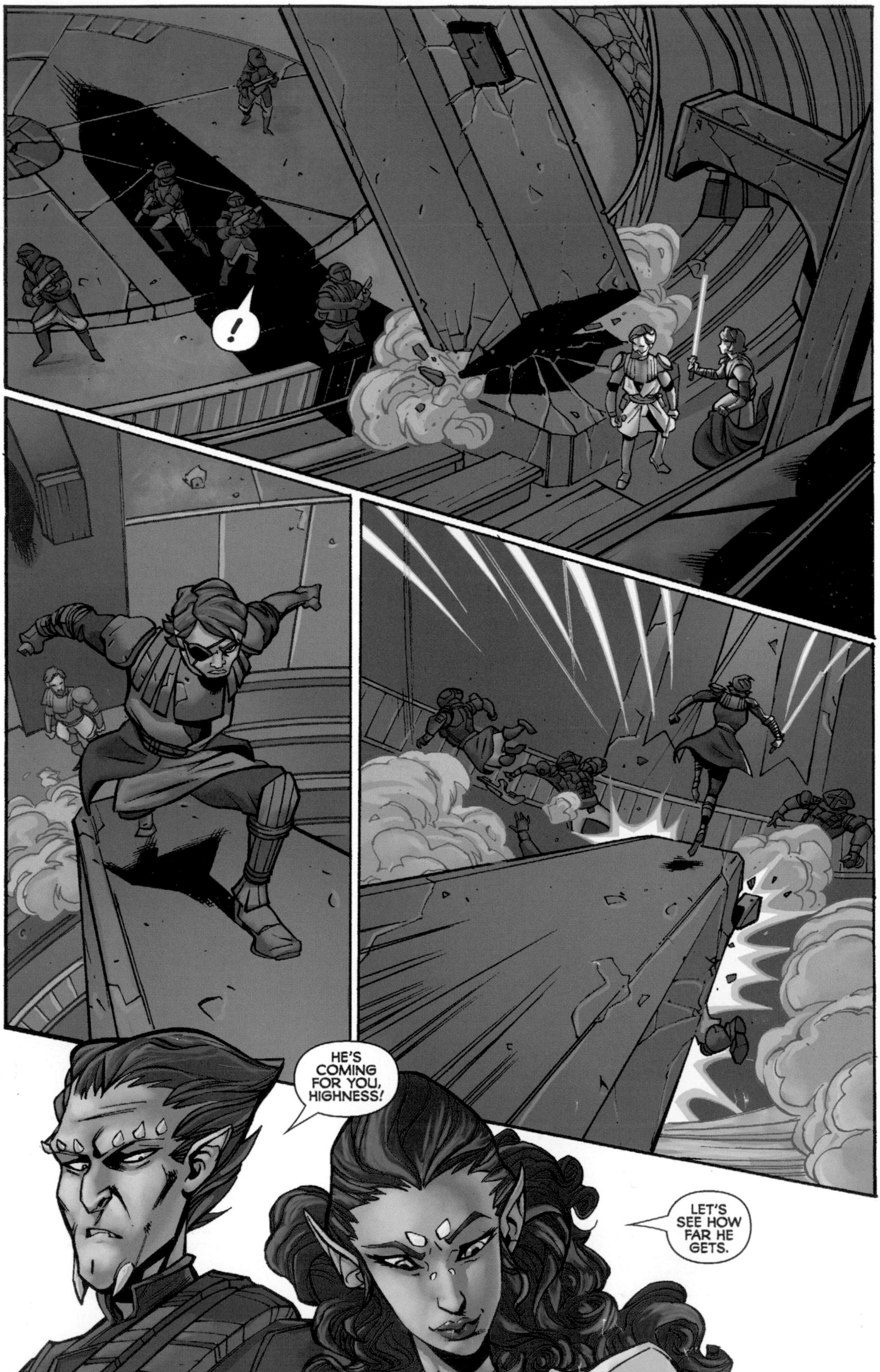
!
HE'S COMING FOR YOU, HIGHNESS!
LET'S SEE HOW FAR HE GETS.

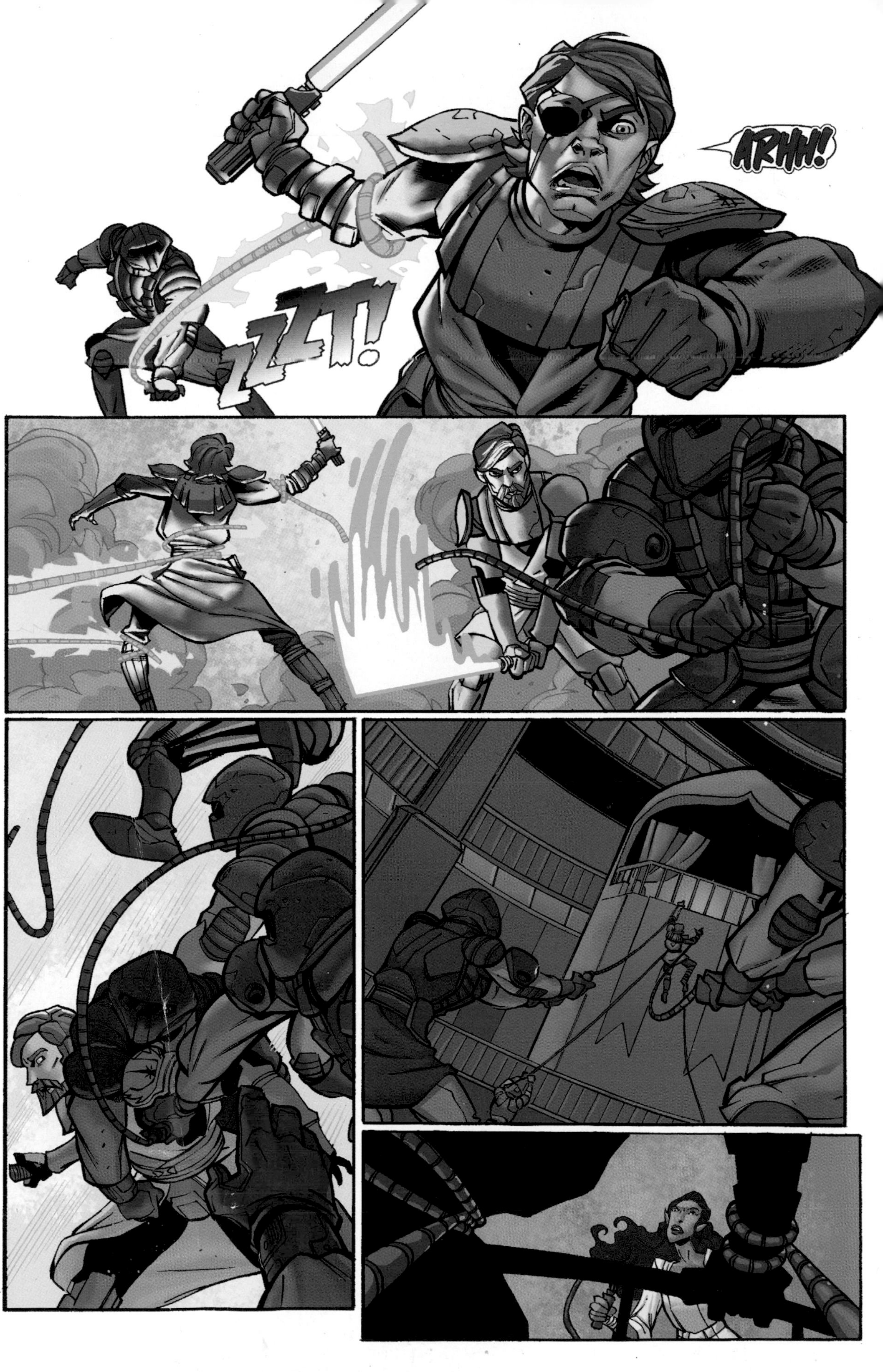
ARHH!
ZZZT!

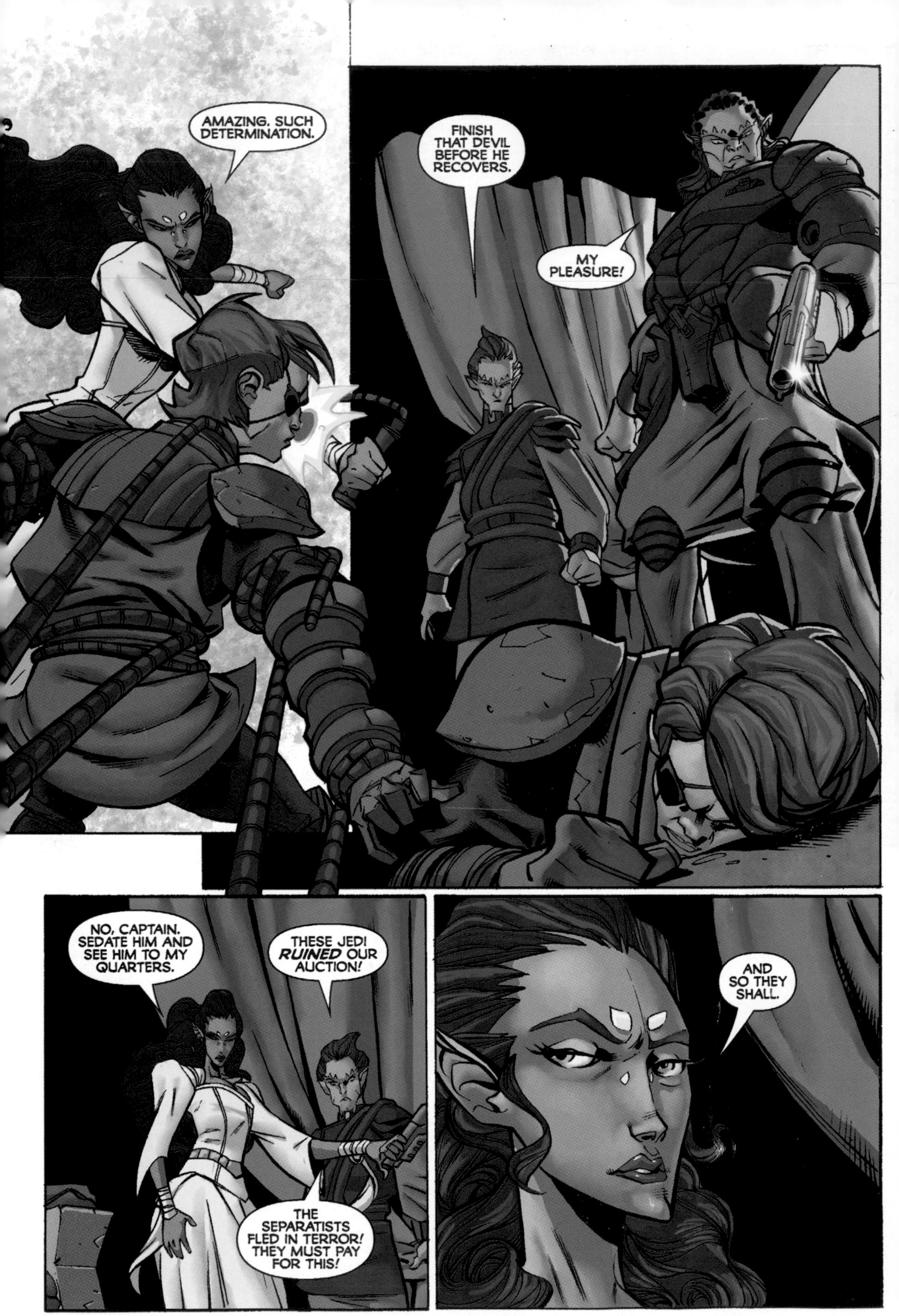
AMAZING. SUCH DETERMINATION.
FINISH THAT DEVIL BEFORE HE RECOVERS.
MY PLEASURE!
NO, CAPTAIN. SEDATE HIM AND SEE HIM TO MY QUARTERS.
THESE JEDI *RUINED* OUR AUCTION!
THE SEPARATISTS FLED IN TERROR! THEY MUST PAY FOR THIS!
AND SO THEY SHALL.

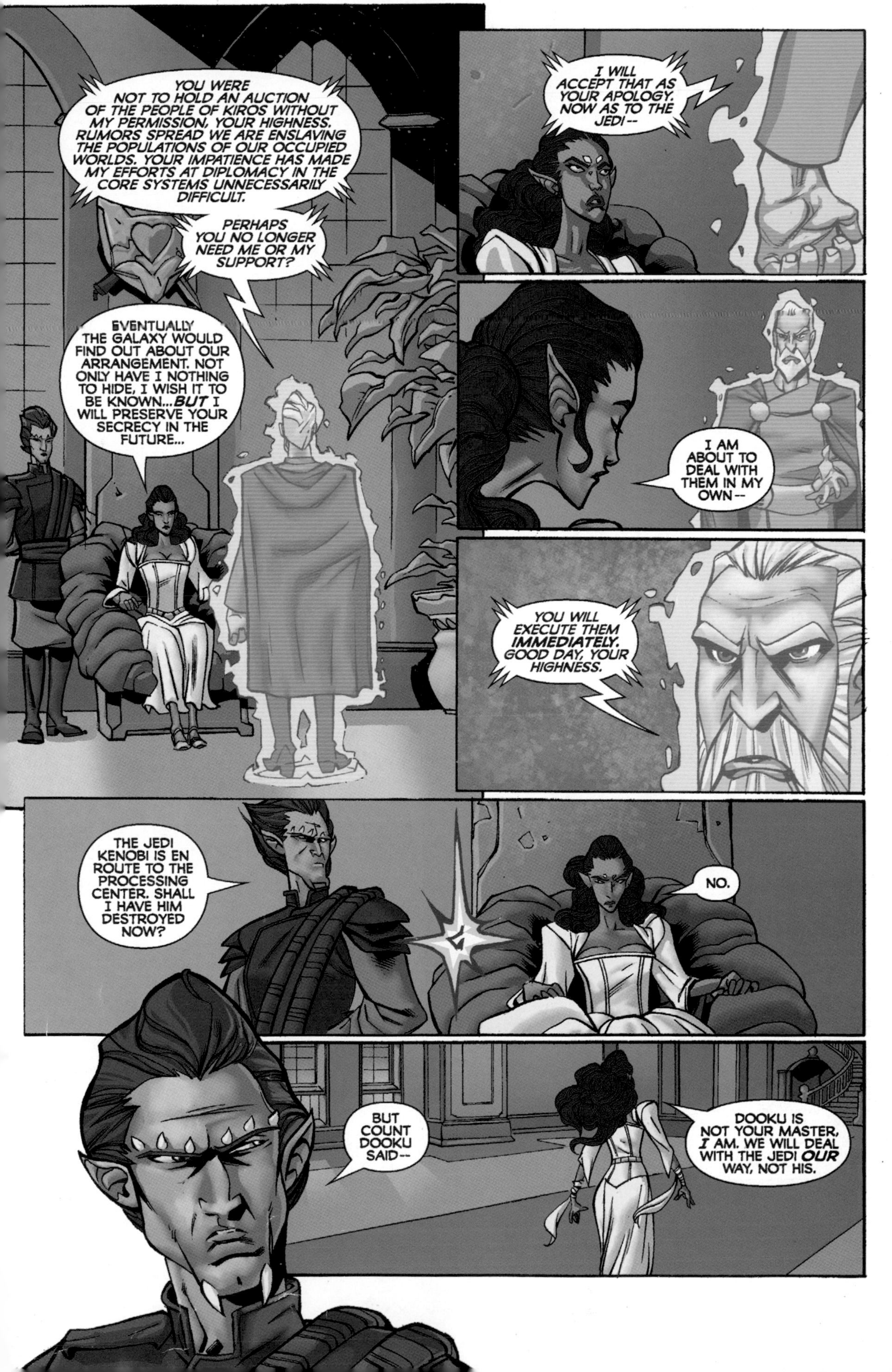
YOU WERE NOT TO HOLD AN AUCTION OF THE PEOPLE OF KIROS WITHOUT MY PERMISSION, YOUR HIGHNESS. RUMORS SPREAD WE ARE ENSLAVING THE POPULATIONS OF OUR OCCUPIED WORLDS. YOUR IMPATIENCE HAS MADE MY EFFORTS AT DIPLOMACY IN THE CORE SYSTEMS UNNECESSARILY DIFFICULT.
PERHAPS YOU NO LONGER NEED ME OR MY SUPPORT?
EVENTUALLY THE GALAXY WOULD FIND OUT ABOUT OUR ARRANGEMENT. NOT ONLY HAVE I NOTHING TO HIDE, I WISH IT TO BE KNOWN...BUT I WILL PRESERVE YOUR SECRECY IN THE FUTURE...
I WILL ACCEPT THAT AS YOUR APOLOGY. NOW AS TO THE JEDI--
I AM ABOUT TO DEAL WITH THEM IN MY OWN--
YOU WILL EXECUTE THEM IMMEDIATELY. GOOD DAY, YOUR HIGHNESS.
THE JEDI KENOBI IS EN ROUTE TO THE PROCESSING CENTER. SHALL I HAVE HIM DESTROYED NOW?
NO.
BUT COUNT DOOKU SAID--
DOOKU IS NOT YOUR MASTER, I AM. WE WILL DEAL WITH THE JEDI OUR WAY, NOT HIS.

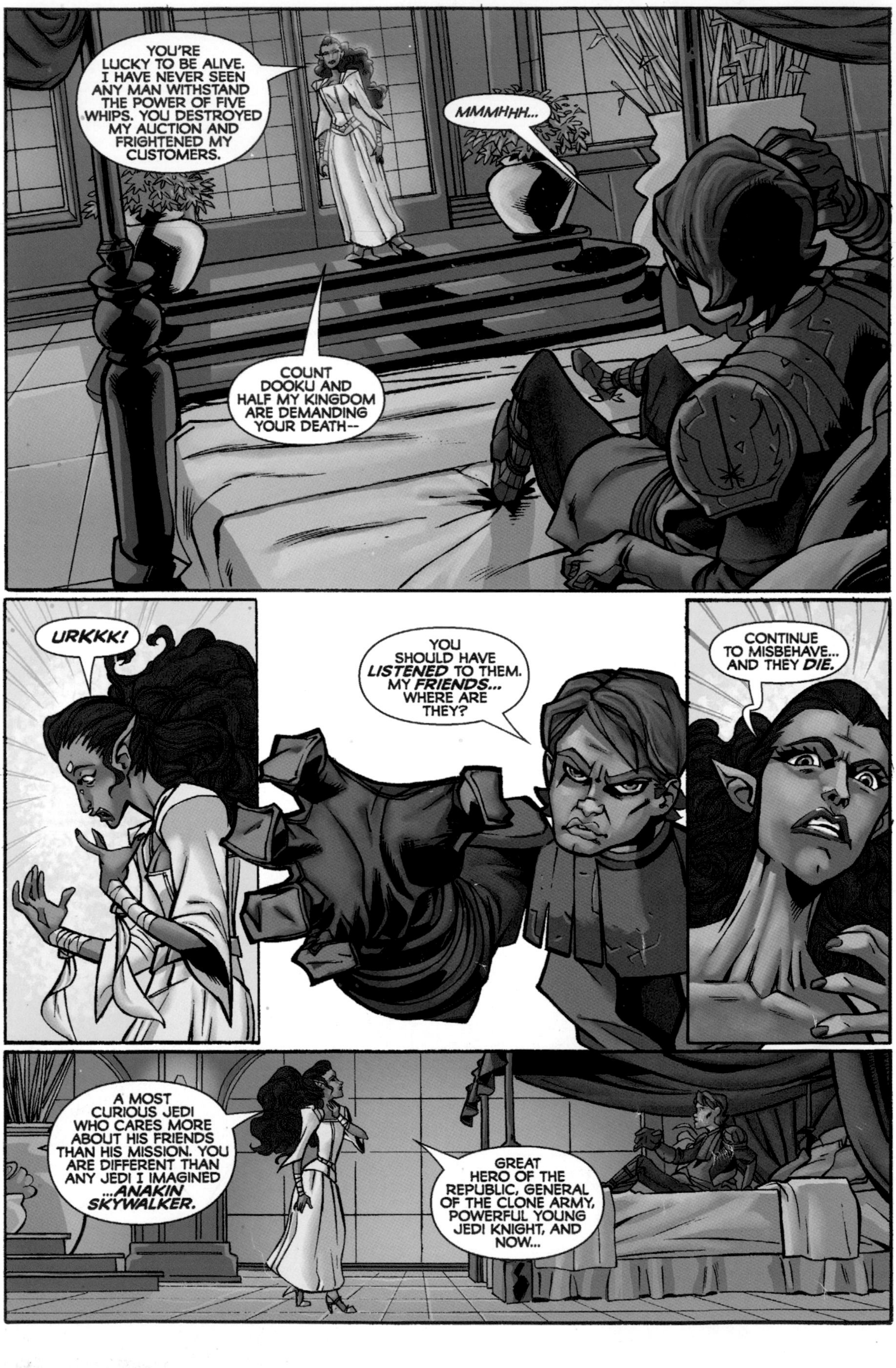

YOU'RE LUCKY TO BE ALIVE. I HAVE NEVER SEEN ANY MAN WITHSTAND THE POWER OF FIVE WHIPS. YOU DESTROYED MY AUCTION AND FRIGHTENED MY CUSTOMERS.
MMMHHH...
COUNT DOOKU AND HALF MY KINGDOM ARE DEMANDING YOUR DEATH--
URKKK!
YOU SHOULD HAVE *LISTENED* TO THEM. MY *FRIENDS...* WHERE ARE THEY?
CONTINUE TO MISBEHAVE... AND THEY *DIE.*
A MOST CURIOUS JEDI WHO CARES MORE ABOUT HIS FRIENDS THAN HIS MISSION. YOU ARE DIFFERENT THAN ANY JEDI I IMAGINED ...*ANAKIN SKYWALKER.*
GREAT HERO OF THE REPUBLIC, GENERAL OF THE CLONE ARMY, POWERFUL YOUNG JEDI KNIGHT, AND NOW...

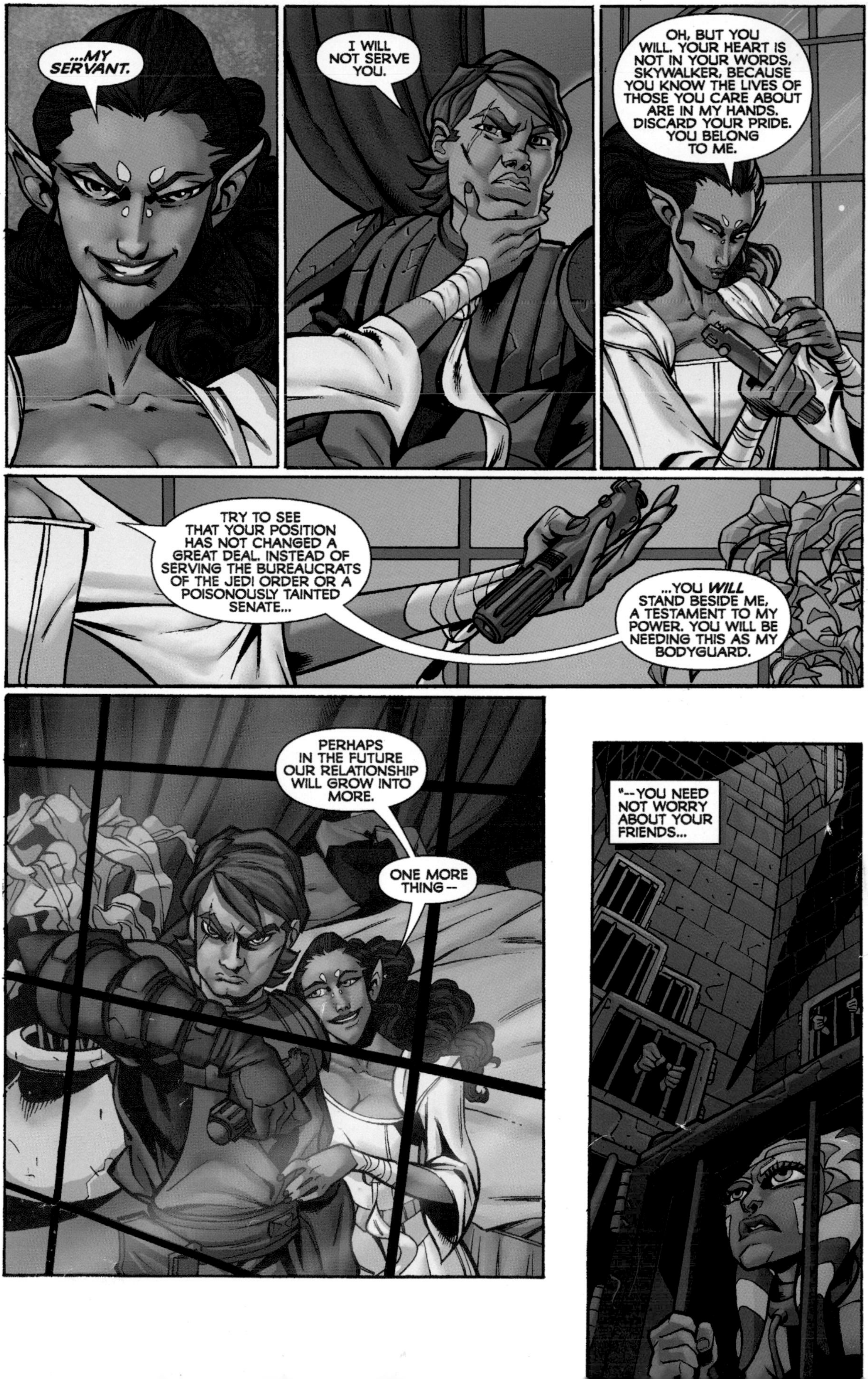
...MY SERVANT.
I WILL NOT SERVE YOU.
OH, BUT YOU WILL. YOUR HEART IS NOT IN YOUR WORDS, SKYWALKER, BECAUSE YOU KNOW THE LIVES OF THOSE YOU CARE ABOUT ARE IN MY HANDS. DISCARD YOUR PRIDE. YOU BELONG TO ME.
TRY TO SEE THAT YOUR POSITION HAS NOT CHANGED A GREAT DEAL. INSTEAD OF SERVING THE BUREAUCRATS OF THE JEDI ORDER OR A POISONOUSLY TAINTED SENATE...
...YOU *WILL* STAND BESIDE ME, A TESTAMENT TO MY POWER. YOU WILL BE NEEDING THIS AS MY BODYGUARD.
PERHAPS IN THE FUTURE OUR RELATIONSHIP WILL GROW INTO MORE.
ONE MORE THING --
"--YOU NEED NOT WORRY ABOUT YOUR FRIENDS...

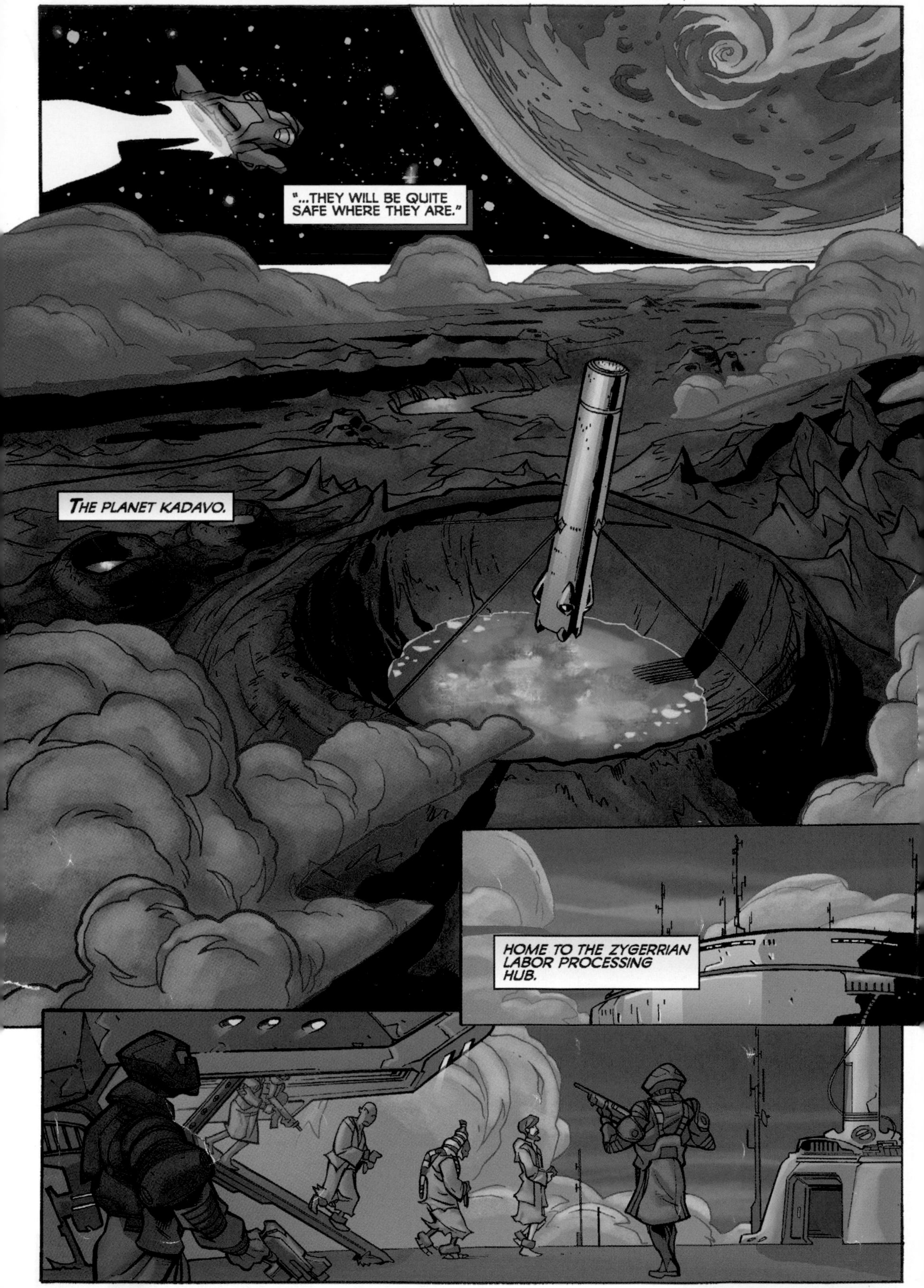
"...THEY WILL BE QUITE SAFE WHERE THEY ARE."
THE PLANET KADAVO.
HOME TO THE ZYGERRIAN LABOR PROCESSING HUB.

next issue:
A SLAVE NOW, A SLAVE FOREVER!